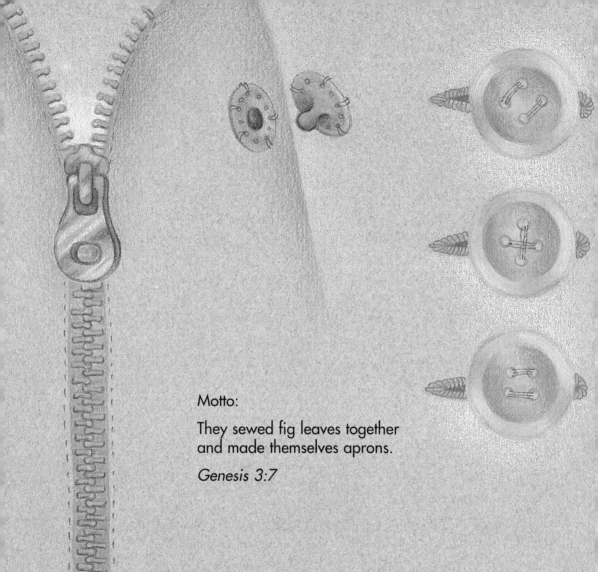

Motto:

They sewed fig leaves together
and made themselves aprons.

Genesis 3:7

Joshua's Book of Clothes

Written and illustrated by Alona Frankel

HarperFestival®
A Division of HarperCollinsPublishers

Hello! I am Joshua's mother.
I want to tell you about Joshua
and about what he wears,
when he gets dressed,
and why he puts on clothes.

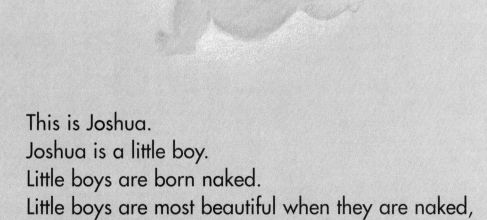

This is Joshua.
Joshua is a little boy.
Little boys are born naked.
Little boys are most beautiful when they are naked,
but they can't be naked all the time.

On bright summer days,
we have to protect our bodies
from the rays of the sun.

On cold days we have to cover
our bodies to keep them warm.
That's why people wear clothes.

People did not always wear the type of clothes
they wear today.

Ages and ages ago, cavemen wore furs.

In ancient Egypt, people wore white linen clothing.

Long ago, in Greece and Rome, people used to wear
long white robes called togas.

In the middle ages in Europe, people wore long, pointy shoes.

And during the Renaissance people dressed up
in fancy velvet clothes and feather hats.

The wide-hooped dresses of the Rococo period
were called crinolines.

And a hundred years ago, men wore tall top hats.

And what does Joshua wear?

Does he wear feathers?

No!
The bird wears feathers.

Is Joshua covered with scales?

No!
The fish is covered with scales.

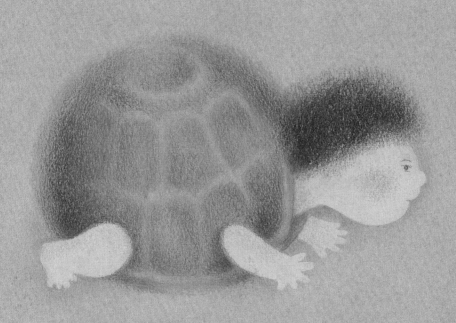

Does Joshua have a shell?

No!
The turtle has a shell.

Joshua wears clothes.

When Joshua was tiny he had tiny clothes,
tiny caps, tiny socks, and tiny shoes.
And I, his mother, would dress him.

Now Joshua has all kinds of clothes,

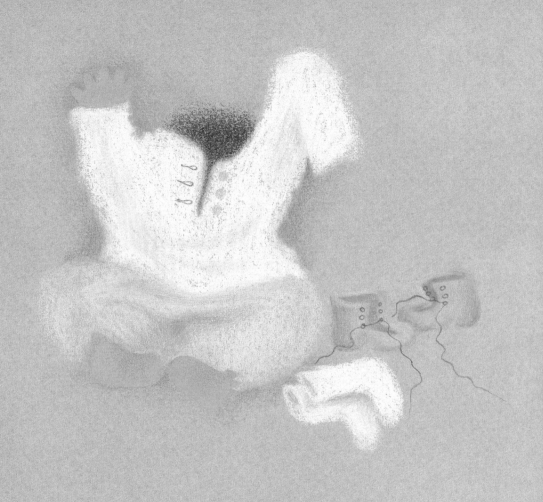

and he can get dressed all by himself.

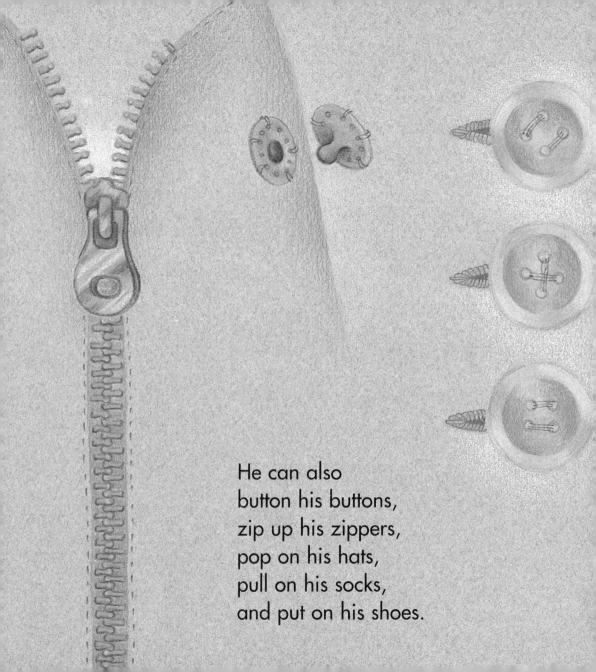

He can also
button his buttons,
zip up his zippers,
pop on his hats,
pull on his socks,
and put on his shoes.

And it is only his shoelaces that I,
Joshua's mother, gladly tie for him.

Joshua has summer clothes which are thin and light.
Light clothing is woven from threads.

Threads are made from plants like flax and cotton.
People can also make threads in factories.

These are Joshua's winter clothes.
They are made of thick, warm materials.

Thick, warm materials are often woven
from the wool of animals like sheep.
Sheep don't mind if you shear off some of their wool,
because it grows back quickly.

Joshua has T-shirts and underwear,
and lots and lots of socks.

Joshua also has many shoes:
sandals for summer, flip-flops for the beach,
boots for winter, sneakers for running and jumping,
tall rubber boots for wading in puddles,
and soft slippers for home.

These are Joshua's hats: a warm hat with flaps
protects his head and ears on cold winter days,
and a summer hat with a brim
protects his face from the sun's rays.

Joshua also has special clothes.

When going to the beach,
he wears a bathing suit.

When playing sports, he wears a sports uniform.

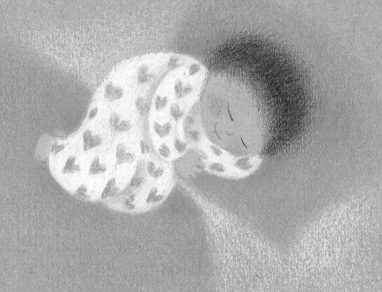

And what does Joshua wear at night?

At night Joshua wears pajamas!

People don't wear the same clothes all over the world.
In parts of Africa it is so hot that some people there
wear very few clothes.

In Alaska it is so cold that the Eskimos there
wear thick, warm furs.

Traditional Japanese women's clothing is the kimono.
In Mexico, a person might wear a wide sombrero
to shade himself from the noonday sun.

American Indians used to wear moccasins on their feet,
and some still do on special occasions.
And Polish girls often weave colored ribbons
into their braids when they dress up for holidays.

Russian traditional clothing includes embroidered shirts,
and in Hawaii it is a custom to wear skirts made of grass.
The Dutch people made wooden clogs popular,
and men in the Scottish Highlands often wear tartan kilts.

f you like all of these beautiful clothes, you can wear them too.
When? At Halloween, of course!

How wonderful!

Alona Frankel
is the author and
illustrator of over thirty titles
for children, including the well-
known Once Upon a Potty.
She is the recipient of
numerous awards, and her books
and art are seen all around the world.
Ms. Frankel lives in Tel Aviv, Israel.

Find out more about Alona
Frankel on the internet at:
www.alonafrankel.com